Feathertop:
A Moralized Legend

*A Whimsical and Haunting Tale of
Illusion, Vanity, and Identity*

A Modern Translation

Adapted for the Contemporary Reader

Nathaniel Hawthorne

Translated by Tim Zengerink

Table of Contents

Preface - Message to the Reader

What If You Could Help Rebuild the Greatest Library in Human History?

Thousands of years ago, the Library of Alexandria stood as the crown jewel of human achievement — a sanctuary where the collected wisdom of every known civilization was gathered, preserved, and shared freely.

And then, it was lost.

Through fire, conquest, and the slow erosion of time, humanity lost not just books — but ideas, dreams, discoveries, and stories that could have changed the world forever.

Today, the Library of Alexandria lives again — and you are invited to be a part of its restoration.

Our mission is simple yet profound:

To rebuild the greatest library the world has ever known, and to translate all timeless works into every language and dialect, so that no seeker of knowledge is ever left behind again.

By joining our movement to rebuild the modern Library of Alexandria, you become part of an unprecedented mission:

- **Unlimited Access to the Greatest Audiobooks & eBooks Ever Written:**

  Instantly explore thousands of legendary works—Plato, Shakespeare, Jane Austen, Leo Tolstoy, and countless more. All instantly available to read or listen, placing a complete literary universe at your fingertips.

- **Beautiful Paperback & Deluxe Editions at Printing Cost**

  Own any title as an elegant paperback, deluxe hardcover, or stunning collectible boxset—offered to you at true printing cost, delivered straight to your door. Build your personal Library of Alexandria, crafted for beauty, built for durability, and worthy of proud display.

- **Fresh Translations for Modern Readers—in Every Language & Dialect**

  Enjoy timeless masterpieces reimagined in clear, contemporary language—no more outdated phrases or obscure references. Alongside the original versions, we're tirelessly translating these classics into every language and dialect imaginable, ensuring accessibility and understanding across cultures and generations.

- **Join a Global Renaissance of Literature & Knowledge**

  You directly support expanding our library, publishing deluxe editions at true cost, translating works into all global languages, and bringing humanity's greatest stories to people everywhere. By joining today, you're not just preserving a legacy of masterpieces; you set in motion a powerful wave of literary accessibility.

Become a Torchbearer of Knowledge.

Join us for free now at **LibraryofAlexandria.com**

Together, we will ensure that the light of human wisdom never fades again.

With gratitude and a shared love of knowledge,

The Modern Library of Alexandria Team

Visit:

www.libraryofalexandria.com

Or scan the code below:

Introduction

Masks, Illusion, and the Mirror of Identity

Nathaniel Hawthorne's short story Feathertop—first published in 1852—offers a witty, satirical, and ultimately haunting exploration of identity, self-deception, and the nature of morality. It is one of his most allegorical and accessible tales, built on the framework of a whimsical fantasy about a witch bringing a scarecrow to life. But beneath its folkloric charm lies a powerful meditation on vanity, performance, and the human struggle to reconcile inner emptiness with outward appearances.

Set in colonial New England, Feathertop follows the titular character, a scarecrow who is magically animated by a witch named Mother Rigby. She dresses him in fine clothes, gives him a pipe to animate his body, and sends him into society under the illusion of being a fashionable gentleman. As Feathertop enters the world of humans—particularly the realm of courtship and social appearances—he is met not with suspicion, but with admiration. No one sees the absurdity of his existence until he himself glimpses his true nature in a mirror. That moment of self-recognition—of seeing the scarecrow beneath the silk—is both his undoing and his liberation.

This introduction examines Feathertop through three key dimensions: its place within Hawthorne's broader philosophical and moral landscape; its use of illusion and theatricality as metaphors for identity and social pretense; and its enduring relevance in today's image-driven, appearance-obsessed culture. Although short and deceptively light in tone, Feathertop delivers a potent moral critique of the masks we wear and the selves we hide—even from ourselves.

Hawthorne's Moral Vision and the Legacy of Puritanism

To understand Feathertop in its fullest context, one must first recognize Nathaniel Hawthorne's lifelong preoccupation with morality, sin, and the Puritan legacy of early America. Hawthorne, a descendent of one of the Salem witch trial judges, carried with him an acute awareness of inherited guilt and the psychological burdens of rigid moral systems. Much of his fiction is concerned with what lies beneath the surface—beneath social customs, religious piety, and public virtue.

In Feathertop, however, Hawthorne takes a more playful route into these serious themes. The tale begins with Mother Rigby, a witty and self-aware witch who acts more like a fairy godmother than a malevolent sorceress. Her decision to create Feathertop is framed as an amusing experiment, a satire on human vanity. Yet her spell, which animates the scarecrow through the use of a pipe, is telling. The breath that animates Feathertop is both literal and symbolic—a puff of smoke, a fleeting illusion. He exists only as long as the deception is maintained.

This magical artifice is central to the story's moral critique. Hawthorne does not attack evil directly, but the complacency and self-delusion that allow evil—or emptiness—to pass as substance. Feathertop is a mirror not just for himself, but for the society that embraces him. His handsome clothes and courtly manners are enough to win social favor, even love. No one questions the depth of his soul—because everyone is equally invested in appearances. Hawthorne, always a skeptic of public morality, presents a world where the external trappings of gentility conceal inner hollowness.

Mother Rigby's final reflection underscores this theme: "There are thousands upon thousands of coxcombs and charlatans in the world, made up of just such a jumble of worn-out, forgotten, and good-for-nothing trash as he was!" In other words, Feathertop is not the exception—he is the rule. Society rewards illusions, and punishes those who confront uncomfortable truths. In this sense, Feathertop's collapse is not a failure, but a rare moment of moral clarity in a world that thrives on deceit.

Theatricality, Performance, and the Self

Feathertop is a story built around performance. From the moment he is brought to life, the scarecrow is cast in a role: gentleman, suitor, man of society. He is dressed, taught to speak, and given a mission. Like an actor sent onstage, he plays his part with surprising success. The other characters—including Polly Gookin, the judge's daughter—respond to his performance with admiration and affection. They see what he projects. And in a world where perception often overrides substance, that projection is enough.

But Hawthorne, ever attuned to the psychological dimensions of character, introduces a crucial moment of rupture. When Feathertop sees his reflection in the mirror and discovers the truth of what he is, the illusion shatters—not only for him but for the reader. This is the turning point of the story, the moral crux. The mirror does not lie. It forces Feathertop to confront what no one else has bothered to see: his inner void.

What follows is not melodrama, but quiet tragedy. Feathertop does not rage or lash out. He returns home, lays down his pipe, and ceases to exist. This act is significant. It is not merely a death—it is a renunciation. He refuses to live as a lie. In doing so, Feathertop becomes the most human character in the story. His capacity for self-awareness, his horror at his own falseness, elevates him above those who continue to live hollow lives without ever facing the truth.

In this way, Feathertop can be read as a parable about the cost of authenticity. The courage to see oneself clearly, and to reject falsehood, comes at a price. Hawthorne suggests that while most people are content to play roles, the truly moral individual cannot live in illusion once it has been unmasked. It is a bleak but bracing vision—one that questions whether society truly values integrity, or whether it rewards only those who can maintain the best performance.

Relevance in the Age of Image and Illusion

Though written in the mid-19th century, Feathertop feels remarkably timely in the 21st. In an era dominated by social media, curated personas, and surface-level branding, the story's themes resonate with new urgency. Today, as in Hawthorne's time, society often mistakes appearance for reality. What is visible, shareable, or aesthetically pleasing is too often equated with truth. In this context, Feathertop becomes a symbol not of the past, but of the present—a prototype of the influencer, the public figure, the viral identity.

What makes Feathertop especially compelling is its refusal to offer easy answers. It does not mock its protagonist, nor does it idealize the society that embraces him. Instead, it draws a circle of irony around both. Feathertop is not evil—he is empty. And society does not care—so long as he looks the part. This dynamic calls into question the foundations of reputation, love, and social value. What do we praise, and why? What are we willing to see, and what do we choose to ignore?

At its core, the story asks a deeply unsettling question: What if there is nothing beneath the mask? And what happens when the mask is removed?

Feathertop's journey—from creation to collapse— is a moral arc not of failure, but of enlightenment. His downfall is, paradoxically, his redemption. He chooses truth over illusion, silence over pretense, self-erasure over self-deception. In doing so, he becomes a rare figure of dignity in a world built on vanity.

As you read this modern translation of Feathertop, consider the ways in which we all participate in illusions. Reflect on the roles we play, the faces we present, the truths we suppress. Hawthorne's scarecrow is not merely a figure of fantasy. He is, in many ways, the most honest character in the room.

And perhaps that, more than any spell or curse, is what makes him truly human.

Feathertop: A Moralized Legend

"Dickon!" Mother Rigby called. "Bring me a coal for my pipe!"

She already had the pipe between her lips, packed with tobacco, but she hadn't bothered to light it. There was no fire in the hearth that morning. But the moment she spoke, the bowl of the pipe glowed red, and a puff of smoke rose from her mouth. No one ever figured out where the coal came from or how it got there—some invisible hand must've done it.

"Perfect," said Mother Rigby with a nod. "Thanks, Dickon! Stay nearby in case I need more help."

She had gotten up early—before sunrise—to make a scarecrow for her cornfield. It was late May, and the crows and blackbirds had already found the tiny green shoots of corn pushing through the soil. She wanted the scarecrow finished right away, ready to start its job that very morning.

Now, Mother Rigby was known far and wide as one of the most clever and powerful witches in New England. If she wanted, she could've made a scarecrow so terrifying it would scare the preacher himself. But she had woken up in a good mood, and the tobacco had made her feel even better, so she decided to make something fancy and impressive instead of scary and ugly.

"I don't want some monster standing in my cornfield, right outside my front door," she said to herself, blowing smoke. "Sure, I could do that if I wanted to—but I'm tired of doing strange and magical things. This time, I'll keep it simple. And there's no reason to frighten all the neighborhood kids, even if I am a witch."

So she decided the scarecrow would look like a gentleman—a fancy man from the city—as much as her materials would allow. Here's what she used to build him:

The most important part, even if it didn't show much, was an old broomstick. Mother Rigby had ridden it through the sky many times at midnight, and now it became the scarecrow's spine—its backbone. One arm was made from a broken flail that her husband had once used before he passed away. The other arm was a mix of a pudding stick and a broken chair leg, tied together loosely at the elbow. For legs, she used a hoe handle on one side and a random stick from the woodpile on the other. His chest and stomach were just a sack filled with straw.

That's the whole body, except for the head. For that, she used a shriveled old pumpkin. She carved two holes for eyes, a slit for a mouth, and left a bluish bump for a nose. It actually looked like a real face.

"I've seen worse heads on real people," she said. "And honestly, some fancy gentlemen don't have much more going on upstairs than this pumpkin."

But what really made the man was the clothing. She pulled down an old purple coat from a peg. It was once fine, made in London with embroidered seams and fancy buttons, though now it was worn out, faded, patched at the elbows, and torn at the edges. There was even a round hole over the heart—either from a ripped-off medal or something worse. People said the coat belonged to the Devil himself, and he left it at Mother Rigby's cottage for when he wanted to show off at fancy dinners.

To match the coat, she added a big velvet vest. It had once been covered with gold leaf designs like October leaves, but that had all faded now. Next, she gave the scarecrow a pair of bright red pants. They had belonged to a French governor long ago and had even touched the steps of King Louis the Great's throne. The pants had been passed from a Frenchman to an Indian shaman, then traded to Mother Rigby for a bit of strong liquor.

She also found a pair of silk stockings and pulled them onto the figure's legs. They were so thin they looked like a dream—and you could clearly see the rough wood underneath through the holes.

Finally, she placed her dead husband's old wig on the pumpkin's head and topped it with a dusty three-cornered hat. She tucked in the longest tail feather from a rooster to finish it off.

Then the old woman stood the scarecrow up in the corner of her cottage and laughed at its yellow face, which had a little bumpy nose stuck proudly in the air. It almost looked full of itself, as if it were saying, "Hey, look at me!"

"And you really are worth looking at!" said Mother Rigby, admiring her own work. "I've made a lot of puppets in my time, but I think this one's the best. He might even be too good to just scare birds. But first, I'll pack myself a fresh pipe of tobacco, and then I'll take him out to the cornfield."

While filling her pipe, Mother Rigby kept staring at the scarecrow with something like motherly pride. Whether it was skill, luck, or straight-up witchcraft, something about the ridiculous figure made it seem oddly human—even dressed in ragged, mismatched clothes. The face, carved into the pumpkin, had a strange grin—somewhere between a smirk and a laugh—as if it knew it was making fun of people. The more she looked at it, the more she liked it.

"Dickon!" she called again. "Bring me another coal for my pipe!"

Just like before, a glowing red coal appeared on top of the tobacco, and she took a deep puff. Smoke drifted out into the golden beam of sunlight coming through the one dusty windowpane. Mother Rigby always liked her pipe lit from a certain special fireplace—wherever that was—and it always came with the help of someone invisible named Dickon.

"That puppet," she thought, eyes still fixed on the scarecrow, "is too good to spend the whole summer standing in a field chasing away birds. He deserves better. Honestly, I've danced with worse-looking fellows at our witch meetings in the woods when there weren't many men around. Maybe I should send him out into the world and let him mix with the rest of those empty-headed people running around out there."

She took a few more puffs from her pipe and smiled.

"He'll fit right in on every street corner," she chuckled. "Well, I wasn't planning to do any real magic today—just light my pipe—but I'm a witch and always will be, so I might as well use my powers. I'll turn this scarecrow into a man, even if it's just for fun!"

As she muttered this, Mother Rigby took the pipe from her mouth and stuck it into the carved mouth of the pumpkin head.

"Puff, my darling, puff!" she said. "Come on, handsome, puff away! Your life depends on it!"

It might sound like a strange thing to say to a pile of sticks, straw, and old clothes with a pumpkin for a head—but remember, Mother Rigby was no ordinary woman. She was a powerful and clever witch. If you keep that in mind, the rest of this story won't seem so impossible.

In fact, the strange part is easier to believe if you accept what happened next: as soon as she told him to puff, the scarecrow blew out a small wisp of smoke. Just a tiny one—but then came another, and another, each one a little stronger.

"Keep puffing, sweetie! That's it, keep going!" she said with a warm smile. "That smoke is your life—trust me."

There's no doubt that the pipe was enchanted. Maybe it was the tobacco, the glowing coal, or the magic smoke—but whatever it was, the spell was working. After a few tries, the scarecrow blew out a thick stream of smoke that floated from the dark corner into the beam of morning sunlight. The smoke twirled and faded into the air.

It looked like it took a lot of effort, because the next few puffs were weaker—even though the coal on the pipe still glowed, lighting up the pumpkin face. Mother Rigby clapped her bony hands and smiled proudly. She could tell the magic was working. The dry, wrinkled pumpkin face started to change. A light mist seemed to drift across it, almost giving it a human look. The image would fade and then return stronger with every puff.

Even the whole body of the scarecrow seemed to come to life, like one of those cloudy shapes we sometimes imagine in the sky—blurry but strangely real.

If you want to be skeptical, you could argue that nothing really changed at all—that it was just an illusion. Maybe it was just clever lighting and shadows playing tricks, making the old scarecrow look alive. Witchcraft often works like that—more tricky than truly magical. But if that explanation doesn't convince you, I don't have a better one to offer.

"Well done, my handsome boy!" Mother Rigby cheered. "Now take another strong puff—put everything you've got into it. Breathe deep like your life depends on it! If you've got a heart in that chest, or even anything close to one, puff from there! Good! You pulled that in like you actually enjoyed it."

Then she motioned to the scarecrow, her gesture full of some strange, invisible power—so strong it felt impossible to resist, like a magnet pulling in metal.

"Why are you just hiding in the corner, you lazy thing?" she said. "Come forward! The whole world is waiting for you!"

Honestly, if I hadn't heard this story from my grandmother when I was a kid—back when I believed anything—I'd have a hard time saying it with a straight face now.

But sure enough, when Mother Rigby spoke and reached toward it, the scarecrow stretched out its arm like it wanted to grab her hand. It took a step—a clumsy, jerking sort of move—and almost fell over. What else could you expect? It was just a scarecrow made of sticks. But the old witch didn't give up. She scowled, motioned again, and poured all her fierce willpower into the thing, as if she could force it to become a real man. And somehow, it worked.

It stepped into the sunlight. There it stood—awkward, shaky, barely held together, like it could collapse any second. It looked more like a bad joke of a person than anything real, a mess of rags and sticks pretending to be human. Honestly, it reminded me of those flat, recycled characters in books—used so many times they've lost all life. (And I say this as someone who's probably written a few myself.)

Mother Rigby, though, was losing patience. A bit of her darker side peeked out—like a snake hissing from her sleeve. She was fed up with how weak and useless the scarecrow seemed after all the work she put into making it.

"Puff, you useless thing!" she yelled. "Puff like your life depends on it, you sack of straw! You rag heap! You empty meal bag! You pumpkin head! You worthless nobody! What can I even call you that's low enough? Puff, I said! Take in that smoke like it's your last chance! If you don't, I'll rip that pipe from your mouth and toss you straight into whatever place that burning coal came from!"

Faced with that threat, the scarecrow had no choice. It puffed for its life. Smoke poured from its mouth in thick clouds, so much that the small cottage filled up with a smoky haze. Only one beam of sunlight managed to slip through, barely outlining the cracked, dusty window across the room.

Mother Rigby stood in the middle of the smoke, one arm on her hip, the other pointing at the scarecrow. She looked like a nightmare come to life—just like when she used to press down on sleeping people's chests and watch them suffer in their dreams. The scarecrow, terrified, kept puffing as hard as it could.

But the effort was working. With each breath of smoke, the scarecrow looked less like a pile of junk and more like a real man. Even its ragged clothes began to change—they looked newer, brighter, with shiny gold threads where they had been torn or faded. And slowly, through the smoke, its face started to come into focus. A yellowish face, dull-eyed, turned toward Mother Rigby.

Finally, she raised her fist and shook it at him. Not because she was truly angry, but because she believed some people only respond to fear. She didn't believe in kindness or hope—not really. Fear was the best motivator she knew. And this was the moment that mattered most. If she couldn't make him do what she wanted now, she planned to tear the whole thing apart and let it go back to being a pile of junk.

"You look like a man," she said coldly. "Now speak like one—even if it's just a weak echo of a real voice. I command you… speak!"

The scarecrow gasped and squirmed a little before finally letting out a soft sound. It blended so much with the smoke from its pipe that it was hard to tell if it was a voice or just another puff. Some storytellers say that Mother Rigby's magic and strong will forced a spirit into the scarecrow, and that spirit was the one speaking.

"Mother," the quiet, smoky voice said, "please don't be so scary! I want to talk, but I don't have a brain— what can I say?"

"You can talk, can't you, sweetheart?" Mother Rigby said, her serious expression melting into a smile. "And now you ask me what to say? You already sound like all those people who talk constantly but never say anything real! Don't worry, once I send you out into the world, you'll have plenty to say. You'll talk as easily as a river flows. Trust me, you've got just enough brain for that!"

"I'm ready to serve you, Mother," said the scarecrow.

"That's more like it," she replied. "You sound just like yourself—sweet, but not saying much. You'll pick up dozens of sayings like that, and hundreds more to go with them. I've put so much effort into making you, and you turned out so well that I love you more than any puppet I've ever created. And I've made them from everything—clay, wax, straw, sticks, fog, mist, sea foam, and chimney smoke. But you're the best. So listen carefully now."

"Yes, dear mother," said the scarecrow. "I'm all ears."

"'With all your heart!'" the old witch laughed, putting her hands on her hips. "What a cute way to say it! And you even touched your chest like there was a real heart in there!"

Pleased and amused by her creation, Mother Rigby told the scarecrow it was time to go out into the world. She said that most people out there weren't any more real than he was. To help him fit in with high society, she gave him a huge fortune. It included a gold mine in a mythical land called Eldorado, ten thousand shares in a worthless company, half a million acres of grape fields at the North Pole, a castle in the clouds, and a fancy home in Spain—with all the money they were supposed to make.

She also gave him the cargo of a sunken ship—salt from Cadiz—that she had magically caused to sink ten years ago. If the salt was still intact and could be brought back, it would sell for a lot. For spending money, she gave him a copper coin from Birmingham—the only real money she had—and a bunch of brass, which she rubbed onto his forehead to make it even shinier.

"With just that brass," said Mother Rigby, "you'll be able to get by anywhere on Earth. Now give me a kiss, my darling! I've done everything I can for you."

To give him one last boost, she gave him a special word to whisper to an important man in the nearby city. This man was a judge, a councilman, a businessman, and a church leader—all in one. The word would serve as his introduction.

"That old man may be stiff with age, but once you whisper this word to him, he'll do whatever you ask," said the witch. "Mother Rigby knows Justice Gookin, and Justice Gookin knows me!"

She leaned in close, her face lit up with excitement as she whispered her next idea.

"Justice Gookin," she said, "has a beautiful daughter. Listen, my dear—you look great, and you're just clever enough to impress people. Once you see how silly others can be, you'll feel even smarter. With your looks and charm, you're the perfect guy to win that girl's heart. Don't question it—I promise it'll happen. Just be bold—sigh, smile, tip your hat, strike a pose like a dancer, put your hand over your chest—and Polly Gookin will be yours!"

The whole time, the scarecrow kept calmly puffing on his pipe, seeming to enjoy it not just because he had to, but because it made him feel good. It was incredible how human he looked. His eyes—yes, he actually seemed to have them—stayed on Mother Rigby, and he nodded or shook his head at the right moments. He even said things like, "Really?", "Is that so?", "You don't say!", and "Oh!"—all the little phrases people use to show they're paying attention or thinking. Even if you had watched him being made, you might believe he truly understood her advice.

The more he smoked, the more alive he seemed. His face looked sharper, his movements more natural, and his voice clearer. His clothes started to shine with fake richness. Even the pipe, which had looked like an old chunk of clay, now looked like a fine, decorated pipe with a painted bowl and an amber tip.

But since his life seemed tied to the smoke, there was a real worry that once the tobacco ran out, he'd stop living. Mother Rigby had thought of that too.

"Hold your pipe, my sweet one," she said, "and I'll fill it again."

It was sad to watch the fancy gentleman fade into a plain scarecrow again while Mother Rigby dumped out the ashes and reached for more tobacco.

"Dickon!" she shouted in her sharp, crackling voice. "Bring me another coal for this pipe!"

As soon as Mother Rigby finished talking, a red glow lit up in the scarecrow's pipe. Without being told, he lifted it to his mouth and took a few short, shaky puffs. Soon, his breathing calmed and became steady.

"Now listen closely, my dear," said Mother Rigby. "No matter what happens, don't ever stop smoking your pipe. Your life depends on it. That's the one thing you truly know. Keep puffing and blowing out the smoke. If anyone asks, tell them it's for your health and that the doctor told you to do it. And when your pipe starts to run out, go somewhere quiet, fill yourself up with smoke, and shout, 'Dickon, more tobacco!' and, 'Dickon, another hot coal for my pipe!' Then get it back into your mouth quickly. If you don't, instead of looking like a fine gentleman in gold-trimmed clothes, you'll turn back into a pile of sticks, rags, straw, and a dried-up pumpkin. Now off you go, my treasure—and good luck!"

"Don't worry, Mother!" the scarecrow said in a strong voice, blowing out a proud puff of smoke. "I'll succeed—if being honest and polite still counts for something!"

"You're going to be the death of me!" laughed the witch so hard she nearly fell over. "That was perfect! You're playing your part like a true gentleman. Go on now, smart boy. I'd bet on you any day—you've got strength, some brains, something like a heart, and everything a man needs. I'm a better witch today just for making you. Didn't I create you myself? I'd like to see any other witch do better! Here, take my staff."

As soon as she handed him the simple wooden stick, it changed into a fancy cane with a golden handle.

"That gold top is just as smart as you are," said Mother Rigby. "It'll lead you straight to Master Gookin's front door. Off you go, my little gem, my sweet, my darling. And if anyone asks your name, it's Feathertop. You've got a feather in your hat, I stuffed feathers into your head, and your wig is the type they call Feathertop—so that's what you'll be called!"

Feathertop left the cottage and walked proudly toward the town. Mother Rigby stood at the door, smiling as the sunlight sparkled on him, making his fancy clothes look even grander. She admired how seriously he puffed his pipe and how nicely he walked, even though his legs were a bit stiff. She watched until he disappeared, then whispered a magical blessing as he turned down the road.

Later that morning, when the town's busiest street was full of life, a tall, elegant stranger walked onto the sidewalk. He looked like someone important. His posture and clothes made him seem like a prince or nobleman. He wore a deep purple coat with golden embroidery, a velvet vest with golden leaves, bright red pants, and shiny white silk stockings. On his head was a carefully styled powdered wig. It looked too perfect to cover with a hat, so he carried his gold-trimmed hat under his arm. A bright star sparkled on his chest. He held his gold-topped cane with style, just like wealthy gentlemen of that time. Delicate lace ruffles at his wrists showed his hands had clearly never done any hard work.

One of the most eye-catching things about him was his pipe. It had a beautifully painted bowl and a smooth amber tip. Every few steps, he took a long breath from it, held it in, then let the smoke flow gracefully from his mouth and nose.

Of course, everyone around was curious to know who this stranger was.

"He must be a nobleman," one man said. "Did you see that star on his coat?"

"It's so bright I could hardly look," said another. "He has to be from royalty. But how did he get here? No ships have arrived from Europe in weeks. And if he came overland, where are his servants and wagons?"

"He doesn't need servants to prove anything," said a third. "Even in torn clothes, you'd still see the nobility in him. I've never seen someone carry themselves like that. He must come from a royal family."

"I think he's German or maybe Dutch," someone else added. "Men from those countries are always smoking."

"Well, so do Turks," said another. "But to me, he looks like someone trained at the French court. Only French nobles have that kind of grace. Look at the way he walks! Some people might think it looks stiff or jerky, but I see true style. He must have studied how the French king moves. I bet he's a French ambassador sent here to talk about Canada."

"Or maybe he's Spanish," said another. "That would explain his yellow skin. He could be from Havana or another Spanish port, sent to check on those pirate rumors people keep talking about. The settlers in Mexico and Peru have skin as gold-colored as the treasures they dig up."

"Yellow or not," said a lady nearby, "he's absolutely handsome! So tall and slim! His face, his perfect nose, that soft smile—he's stunning. And that star—it looks like it's on fire!"

"So do your eyes, beautiful lady," said the stranger, tipping his head and waving his pipe as he passed. "They've truly dazzled me."

"What a charming and original compliment!" the lady whispered, blushing with excitement.

Almost everyone admired the mysterious stranger. But there were two who didn't. One was a small dog, who sniffed around his feet, then ran away yelping in fear. The other was a little child who burst into tears and started shouting something about a pumpkin.

Feathertop continued walking down the street. Aside from a brief compliment to the lady and an occasional polite nod to the people bowing around him, he stayed focused on his pipe. The calm, confident way he carried himself proved he was someone important, even as the growing crowd watched him with curiosity and excitement.

With a group of townspeople following behind, he finally arrived at the grand home of Justice Gookin. He stepped through the gate, climbed the front steps, and knocked on the door. While waiting, he tapped the ashes out of his pipe.

"What did he just say in that sharp voice?" asked someone nearby.

"I'm not sure," said another. "But the sunlight is hurting my eyes. He suddenly looks faded and dull. What's going on with me?"

"The strange thing," said the first, "is that his pipe, which was just out, is burning again—and the coal is glowing redder than ever. There's something strange about this man. Did you see that puff of smoke? You said he looked faded? Look again—his star is glowing like fire!"

"It really is," said his friend. "And look—there's Polly Gookin watching him from the upstairs window. That star might dazzle her for sure."

Just then, the door opened. Feathertop turned to the crowd, gave a proud, formal bow like an important man greeting commoners, and stepped inside the house. He wore a mysterious smile—maybe more of a grin or a strange smirk—but no one in the crowd seemed to notice anything suspicious about him. Only a little child and a barking dog seemed to sense that something wasn't quite right.

From here, the story skips a bit and picks up with Polly Gookin, the judge's daughter. She was a sweet-looking young woman with blonde hair, blue eyes, and a rosy face that didn't seem too clever but not foolish either. She had caught a glimpse of the shiny stranger from the doorway and rushed to get ready. She quickly put on her fancy lace cap, a string of beads, her best scarf, and a stiff damask skirt to impress him.

Since then, she had been standing in front of the big mirror in the parlor, practicing different expressions—smiling sweetly, posing politely, and then smiling again even softer. She also blew kisses, tilted her head, and twirled her fan. In the mirror, her reflection copied everything she did, but she didn't feel embarrassed by it. In fact, it seemed like Polly's own imagination was helping her become just as fake and polished as Feathertop himself. By acting this way, she made herself easier for the enchanted stranger to impress.

Just as Polly heard her father's slow, limping steps coming down the hall—along with the click of Feathertop's fancy high-heeled shoes—she quickly sat upright on the couch and began singing sweetly as if she hadn't been preparing at all.

"Polly! Daughter Polly!" her father called. "Come here, child."

When Justice Gookin opened the door, he looked unsure and a little uneasy.

"This gentleman," he said, introducing Feathertop, "is Chevalier Feathertop—no, I mean, Lord Feathertop—who brings a message from an old friend of mine. Show respect to his lordship, child, and treat him with the honor his status deserves."

Then the judge quickly left the room. But if Polly had taken a moment to glance at her father instead of staring dreamily at her dazzling guest, she might have noticed something was off. Her father was clearly nervous, fidgeting, and pale. He tried to smile politely, but it turned into a strange, twitchy grin. Once Feathertop turned away, the old man scowled, shook his fist, and stomped his aching foot—though this rude gesture brought him no relief.

It seemed that the secret message Mother Rigby had given Feathertop affected the judge more with fear than friendliness. And being a sharp observer, he had noticed something strange: the images on Feathertop's pipe bowl were moving. Looking closer, he realized the decorations were tiny demons—with horns and tails—dancing hand in hand around the edge of the bowl, laughing in a creepy way.

As if that weren't enough, while leading Feathertop through a dark hallway, the star on the scarecrow's chest flickered and gave off real flames, casting eerie light on the walls and floor.

With all these creepy signs, it's no wonder the old judge felt worried about letting his daughter meet such a strange visitor. He hated how charming and smooth Feathertop seemed as he bowed, smiled, put a hand on his heart, took a long breath from his pipe, and let out a smoky sigh into the room. Deep down, the old man probably wished he could throw this mysterious guest out of his house. But he felt powerless and afraid. Maybe, earlier in life, he had made some dark promise—and now he feared he might have to repay it by giving up his daughter.

As it happened, the parlor door was partly made of glass and covered by a silk curtain that was a little off-center. The judge was so anxious about what might happen between Polly and Feathertop that, after leaving the room, he couldn't help peeking through the curtain's edge to watch.

There was nothing truly magical to see—just the small, strange details already mentioned. Nothing clearly showed that Polly Gookin was in real danger. The stranger, to be fair, acted exactly like a calm, confident man who knew how to handle himself. He seemed like the kind of person a parent should keep an eye on around a young, innocent girl.

Justice Gookin, who had met all kinds of people in his life, noticed that Feathertop's every move was practiced and polished. There was nothing natural or honest about him. He didn't seem like a real person at all, but more like a living statue. Everything about him was so perfect it felt fake—so fake, it was almost creepy. He seemed less like a man and more like the smoke from his pipe shaped into a body.

But Polly didn't see him that way. She was completely taken in. They walked slowly around the room—Feathertop with his dramatic steps and fancy expressions, and Polly moving gracefully beside him, picking up just a little of his exaggerated style but still holding on to her natural charm. The longer they spent together, the more enchanted Polly became. Within fifteen minutes (as her father nervously checked his watch), it was obvious she was falling in love.

Maybe it wasn't magic. Maybe her heart was just so ready for love that she poured all her feelings into whoever stood before her, even if he was only a clever illusion. No matter what Feathertop said, it sounded important to her. No matter what he did, it looked brave. Her cheeks were probably blushing, her smile soft and sweet, her eyes dreamy and glowing. Meanwhile, the star on Feathertop's chest kept flashing brightly, and the tiny carvings of dancing demons on his pipe swirled and spun as if celebrating her falling for a fantasy.

But why were they so excited that Polly was about to give her heart to someone who wasn't real? Was it really that rare?

Feathertop suddenly stopped. He stood tall and confident, showing off every part of his sparkling outfit, like he was daring Polly not to fall for him. The star on his chest gleamed, his coat shone, his buckles glinted, and the colors of his clothing looked even richer. He looked like the perfect gentleman. Polly looked up at him shyly, full of admiration. Then she glanced at the large mirror across the room, wanting to see how she looked beside someone so impressive.

The mirror was very clear and honest. It didn't lie.

As soon as Polly saw their reflections, she screamed. She stumbled back in shock, stared at Feathertop in horror, and then fainted right onto the floor. Feathertop had looked too—and what he saw wasn't the elegant man he expected. Instead, the mirror showed what he really was: a bunch of sticks, rags, and a carved pumpkin. All the magic had disappeared.

Poor Feathertop! You couldn't help but feel sorry for him. He raised his arms in despair, and for the first time, his reaction felt truly human. Maybe, just once in this world full of lies and pretending, an illusion had looked in the mirror and fully understood what it was.

That evening, as the sun went down, Mother Rigby sat by her fireplace. She tapped ashes from a fresh pipe when she heard a strange, fast-paced clatter coming down the road. But it didn't sound like footsteps—it sounded more like sticks clacking or dry bones rattling.

"Huh!" she said to herself. "What's that? Which skeleton is out of its grave now?"

The door burst open, and Feathertop ran in! His pipe still glowed, the star on his chest still burned, and his clothes still looked impressive. On the outside, he hadn't changed. But something was different—you could feel that the magic wasn't holding him together anymore.

"What happened?" asked the witch. "Did that fake holy man throw you out? That coward! I'll send a pack of demons after him until he begs you to marry his daughter!"

"No, Mother," Feathertop said quietly. "It wasn't him."

"Did the girl turn you down?" she asked, her eyes burning with rage. "I'll cover her face with pimples! Make her nose red as your pipe! Knock out her front teeth! She'll be too ugly for anyone by next week!"

"Don't blame her, Mother," Feathertop said sadly. "She almost loved me. I think if she had kissed me, I might have truly become human. But..." He paused, then shouted with pain, "I saw myself, Mother! I saw what I really am—just a sad, fake pile of straw! I can't keep pretending!"

He grabbed the pipe from his mouth and threw it hard into the fireplace. It shattered. In the same moment, he collapsed to the ground. What remained was only a heap of straw, torn clothes, a few sticks, and a dried-up pumpkin. The eyes were now empty holes, but the mouth still looked like it was twisted in a final, hopeless grin—almost human.

"Poor thing," muttered Mother Rigby, looking down at the mess she had made. "My poor, sweet, handsome Feathertop. The world is full of fools and fakes made from the same kind of trash he was. And yet, they go on living, pretending, never realizing what they really are. So why did my poor puppet have to be the only one to see the truth—and fall apart because of it?"

As she spoke, she packed more tobacco into a fresh pipe. She held it in her fingers, not sure if she should smoke it herself or bring Feathertop back again.

"Poor Feathertop," she said with a sigh. "I could easily fix him up and send him out again tomorrow. But no—he's too gentle. He feels too much. He has too much heart for such a cold, selfish world. You know what? I'll turn him into a scarecrow instead. That's an honest and useful job. It suits him better. And if every human had a job that truly matched who they were, the world would be a better place. As for this pipe—I think I need it more than he does."

Then she put the pipe between her lips.

"Dickon!" she called out in her sharp voice. "Bring me another coal for my pipe!"

The End

Thank You for Reading

Dear Reader,

We hope this timeless classic has sparked your imagination and enriched your literary journey. Now that you've turned the final page, we want to share a vision for the future of reading—one where every classic you've ever wanted to explore is at your fingertips, in a format that best suits your life.

We'd like to invite you to gain immediate, unlimited digital & audiobook access to hundreds of the most treasured literary classics ever written—along with the option to secure deluxe paperback, hardcover & box set editions at printing cost. Together, we can spark a new global literary renaissance alongside our small, independent publishing house called "The Library of Alexandria."

Thousands of years ago, the Library of Alexandria stood as a beacon of knowledge—until it was lost to history. We aim to reignite that spirit of preservation and discovery right now, in the modern age—only this time, it's accessible to all, in every language and every format.

Picture a world where every timeless classic, novel, poem, or philosophical treatise is not only available to read but also updated for today's readers—modernized, translated into any language or dialect, and ready to enjoy in any format you choose, whether that is in an eBook, audiobook, paperback, or deluxe hardcover & box set version a printing cost.

By joining our movement to rebuild the modern Library of Alexandria, you become part of an unprecedented mission to offer:

- **Unlimited Audiobook & eBook Access to the Greatest Classics of All Time**

    Instantly explore thousands of legendary works, from Plato and Shakespeare to Jane Austen and Leo Tolstoy. All are instantly ready to read or listen to, giving you a complete literary universe at your fingertips.

- **Paperback & Deluxe Editions at Printing Costs:**

    Purchase any title in a paperback, deluxe hardbound, or deluxe boxset edition at printing costs, shipped right to your doorstep. Curate your personal library of Alexandria with editions worthy of display— crafted to last, designed to captivate, and delivered straight to your door.

- **Modern translations for Contemporary Readers in all languages and dialects**

  Discover a vast selection of classics reimagined in clear, current language—no more struggling with outdated phrases or obscure references. Next to the original versions, we aim to offer translations in as many languages and dialects as possible.

  As we continue our translation efforts and add new languages, readers everywhere can connect with these works as if they were written today. By bridging linguistic divides, you're contributing to ensuring that these timeless stories become more meaningful, accessible, and inspiring for people across the globe.

- **Your Personal Library of Alexandria:**

  Over the months and years, you'll curate a unique physical archive of classics—each volume a testament to your taste, curiosity, and love of knowledge. It's not just about owning books—it's about curating a cultural legacy you'll cherish and pass down for generations to come.

- **Join a Global Literary Renaissance:**

  Your support fuels an ongoing mission: allowing us to reinvest in offering deluxe print editions (including special boxsets) at their true cost, broaden the range of available formats and translations, and extend the reach of these works to new audiences worldwide. By joining today, you're not just preserving a legacy of masterpieces; you set in motion a powerful wave of literary accessibility.

We are more than a publisher—we're a movement, and we can't do it alone. Your support lets us scale our mission, preserving and reimagining history's greatest works for tomorrow's readers.

Become a Torchbearer of knowledge.

Thank you for picking up this book and allowing us into your literary journey. As you turn the pages, know that you're part of something larger: a global effort to keep these stories alive, share their wisdom across borders and generations, and spark a true cultural revival for the modern era.

If this resonates with you—please consider taking the next step by visiting:

www.libraryofalexandria.com

With gratitude and a shared love of knowledge,

The Modern Library of Alexandria Team

Visit:

www.libraryofalexandria.com

Or scan the code below:

www.ingramcontent.com/pod-product-compliance
Lightning Source LLC
Chambersburg PA
CBHW011526240626
47154CB00009B/2985